How to Keep a Fairy

Joy McGuire
&
Tom McGuire

Pure Fate Publishing

HOW TO KEEP A FAIRY

Copyright © 2019 by Joy McGuire

ISBN: 978-1-7332350-9-9

All rights reserved. No part of this publication may be reproduced, distributed, or transmitted in any form or by any means, including photocopying, recording, or other electronic or mechanical methods without the prior written permission of the authors, except in the case of brief quotations embodied in critical reviews and certain other noncommercial uses permitted by copyright law.

For the purposes of illustrations for this book, all photos are exclusively of Fae Folk® Fairies and under copyright by Fae Folk World.

Dedicated to Joy's mother, Dorothy June Richmond

As a child she believed in fairies and as an adult she would make us tiny pancakes that we would take to the woods and leave as gifts at the bases of trees.

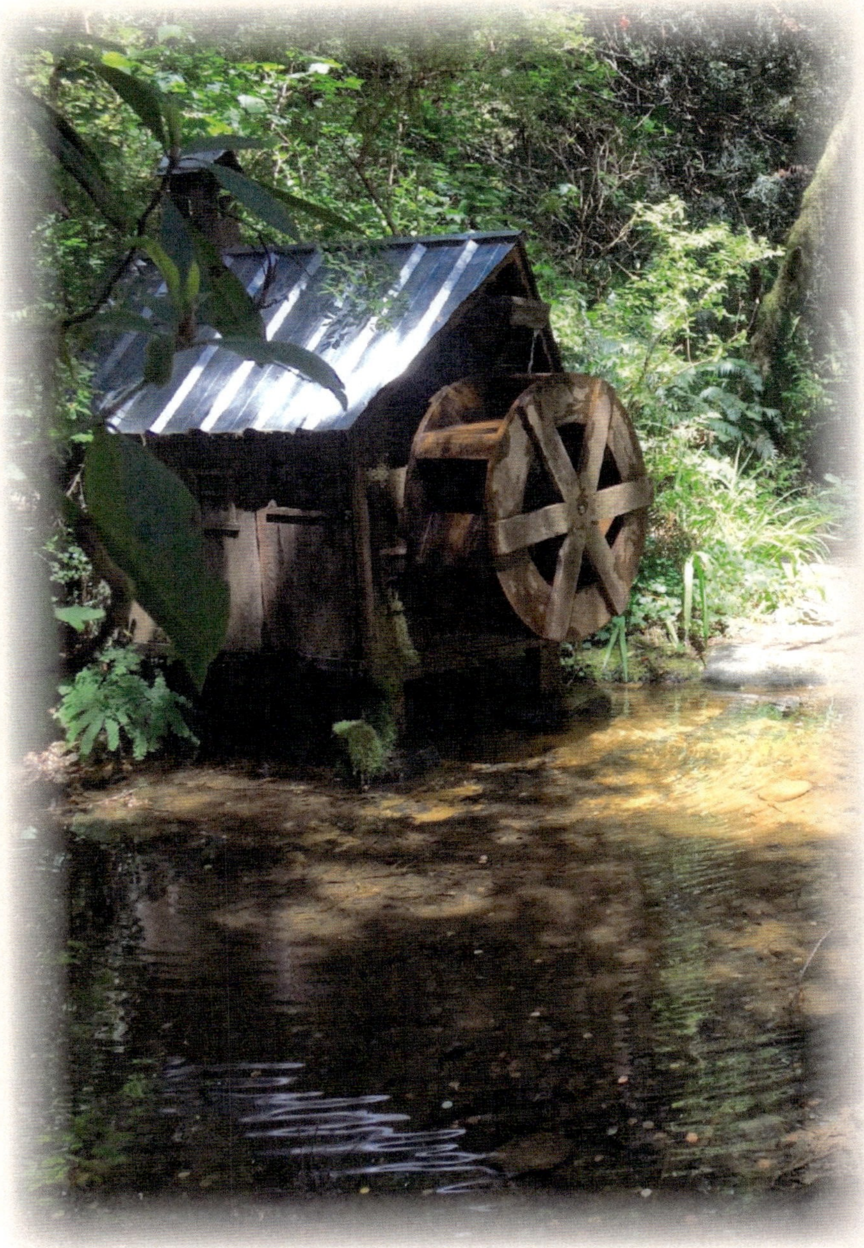

Do you believe...
>In wishing wells,
>And fairy tales,
>And the magic of a starlit night?

Do you believe...
>In Mother Earth,
>And spreading love,
>And doing what you know is right?

Do you believe...
>In nature walks,
>And hidden doors,
>And exploring what's beyond your sight?

Then welcome to the World of the Fae,
Where your imagination is invited out to play.

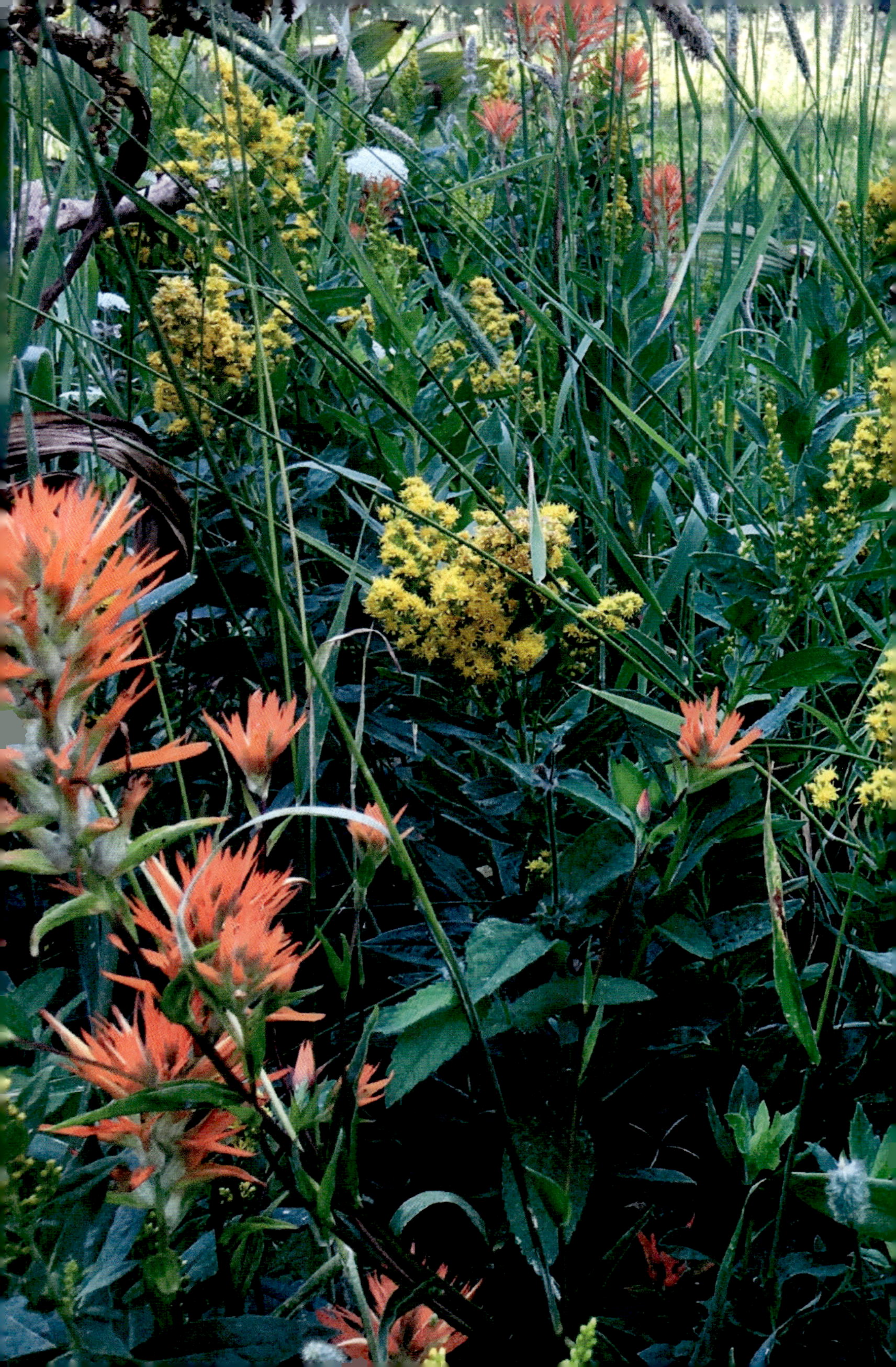

Table of Contents

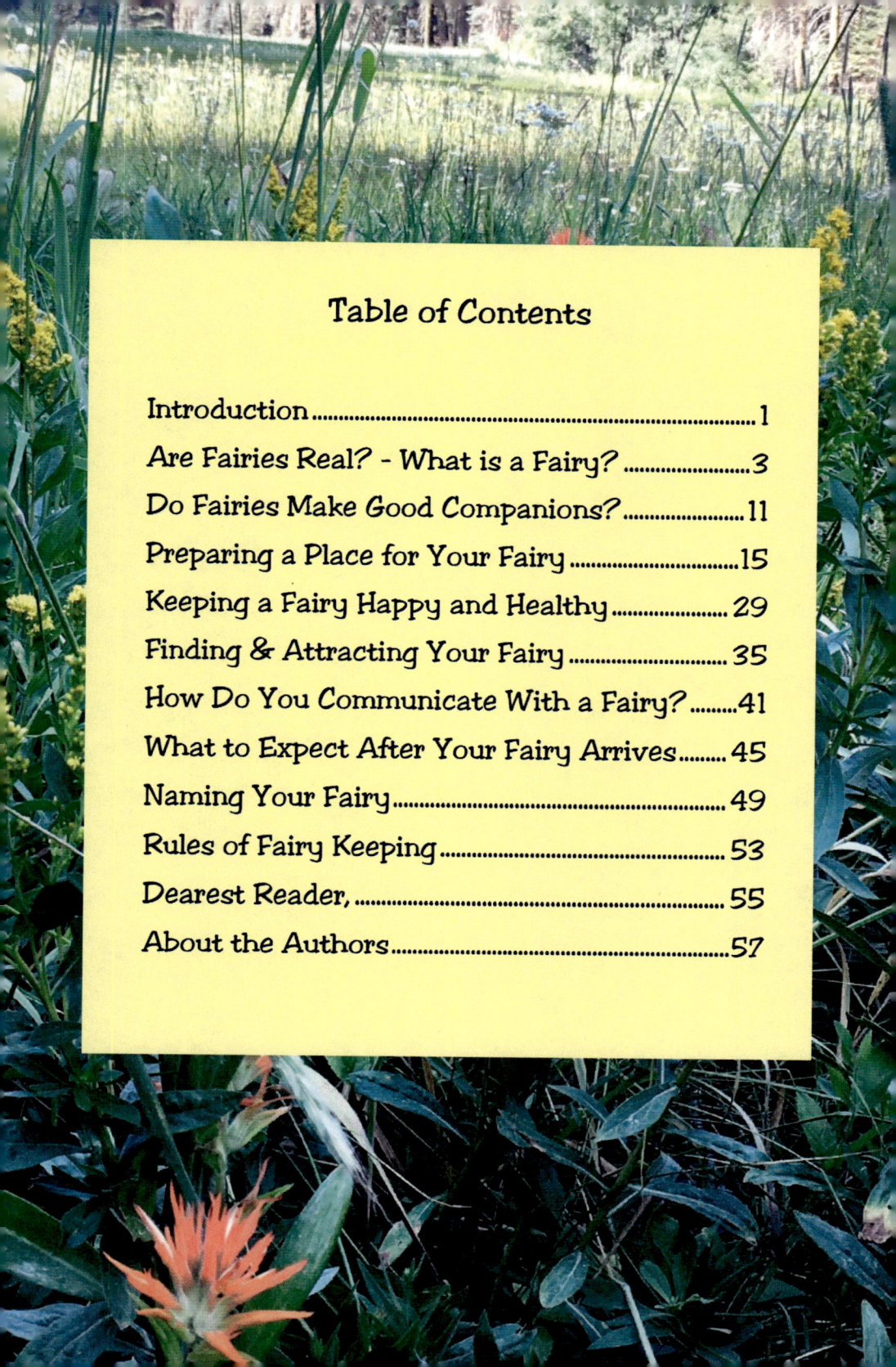

Introduction 1
Are Fairies Real? - What is a Fairy? 3
Do Fairies Make Good Companions? 11
Preparing a Place for Your Fairy 15
Keeping a Fairy Happy and Healthy 29
Finding & Attracting Your Fairy 35
How Do You Communicate With a Fairy? 41
What to Expect After Your Fairy Arrives 45
Naming Your Fairy 49
Rules of Fairy Keeping 53
Dearest Reader, ... 55
About the Authors 57

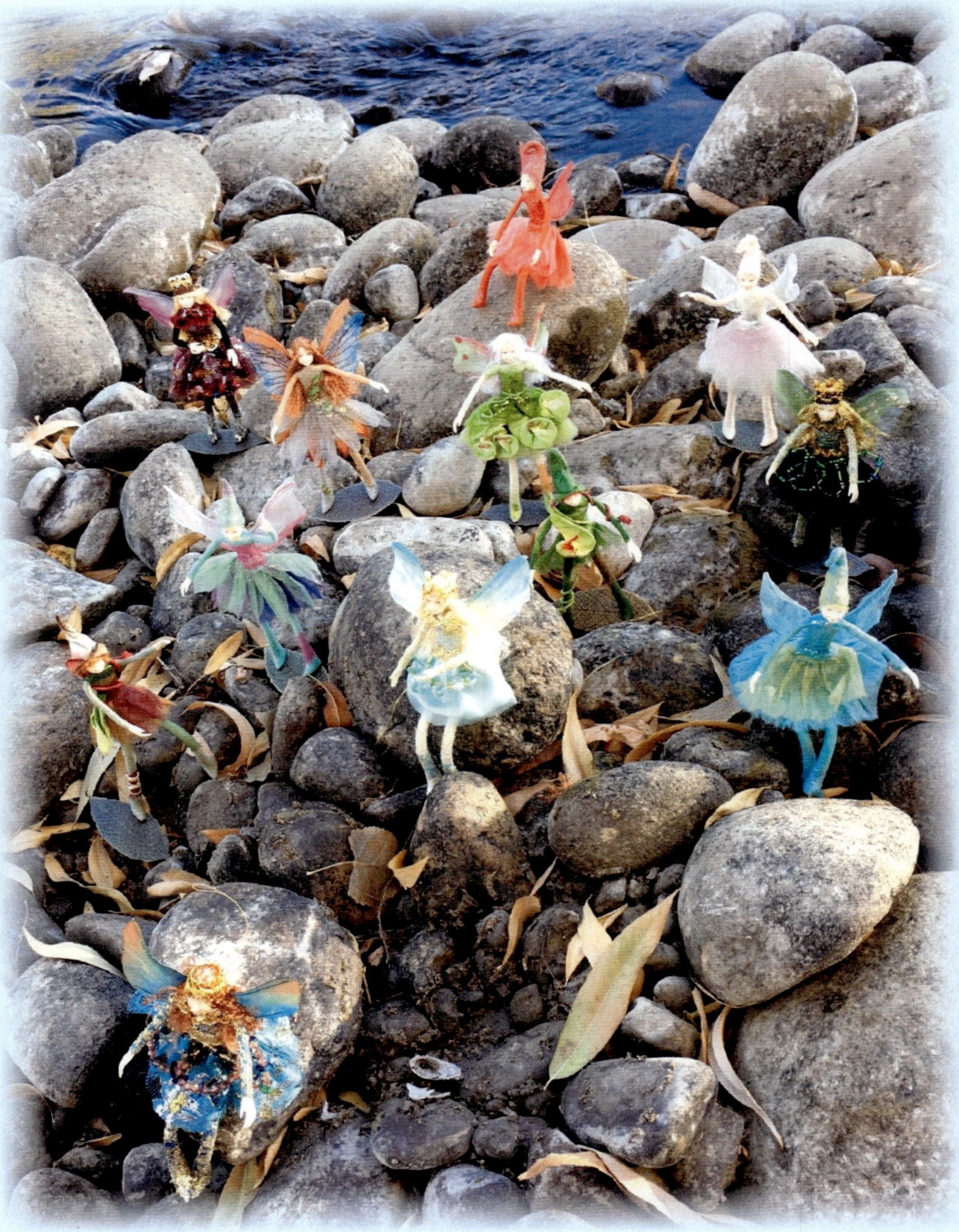

Introduction

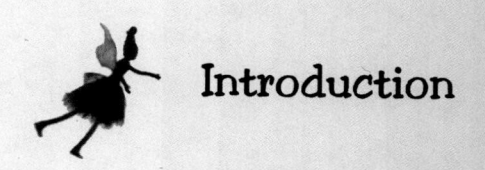

So you've decided to become a fairy keeper. Congratulations! The fact that you're holding this book means that you are interested in doing it right. On behalf of all the wee folk around the world, we thank you!

Maybe you already know a fairy of your very own,

or maybe you're looking to get a fairy friend.

Maybe you're just a friend of the fae and interested in a better understanding.

This book will help in all the above.

> Caution: This book is written to the heart and not the head.

Use your own discernment and intuition while reading. As with all of life, accept those things that ring true with you, and discard those that don't.

- 2 -

Are Fairies Real? - What is a Fairy?

To glimpse a fairy is not very hard,
Just open your heart and let down your guard.

If you look up the word "fairy" in a Merriam-Webster dictionary, you will find this definition: "a mythical being of folklore and romance usually having diminutive human form and magic powers". Not exactly helpful or enlightening, this might as well be a definition of Peter Pan's Tinkerbell!

Worse, further research on the internet may leave you overwhelmed and confused. Even the origin of the word is up for debate. Most agree it comes from the Latin root word fatum, which translates to fate, which is defined as being something beyond control. Ever try to control Mother Nature?

There is even disagreement on spelling. Some use the French form of spelling: Faeries. It's even been suggested that Faeries (with an "e") are "bad" and Fairies (with an "i") are "good". So indeed, there is much confusion.

Fairies can vary in size from taller than humans to as tiny as insects. Some have wings and some do not. Even the physical descriptions have changed throughout the centuries from grotesque to stunning.

Different places around the planet have their own definitions and names for fairies. In Hawaiian culture the little people are the Menehunes. In Ireland, the wee folk are Leprechauns. Culture also plays a big role in whether or not people believe in fairies. In countries such as Iceland, well over fifty percent of the population are still believers.

Media influences beliefs as well. Who hasn't heard of the tooth-fairy, fairy-godmothers, or fairy tales? Santa Claus was famously described as a "jolly old elf" and the most renowned pixie imagery of all time may well be Disney's Tinkerbell.

So "What is a fairy?" depends on a point in time and a place in culture, and there is no one uniform answer.

The common denominator throughout the ages has been that they are beings associated with, and living in, **nature**.

The four elements of nature are air, earth, fire, and water, and there are groups, or species of beings, that are associated with each element.

Air

Fire

Earth

Water

It is hard to name that which cannot be clearly defined, so there have been many names created for these groups or species. Nature Spirits, Gnomes, Wee Folk, Sprites, Nymphs, Elves, Mermaids, Sylphs, Brownies, Pixies, Imps, Trolls,

- 5 -

Elemental Beings, Seelies, and Hobgoblins, are just some of the many names given to these nature beings.

For the purposes of this book, we will be using the generic name of "fairy" to cover the entire group of these ethereal beings.

They are all inter-dimensional beings, able to travel in and out of our human third dimension at will. They exist at a much higher vibration than people do. That is why they may be both seen and unseen, and may change their size and form, and are said to possess magic.

In the distant past fairies were mostly viewed as malevolent and they were to be feared and avoided. Because fairies were associated with nature, to displease a fairy meant your crops may not receive enough water, your home may be destroyed by fire, or your neighbor turned to stone. Scary stuff!

Most of these myths have been disproven with science and fairies have come to be seen as lighthearted creatures. Although they do not live in the world of science: They dwell in the realms of magic.

By magic, we mean the unseen energies that exist everywhere in the universe. Anyone can learn how to harness these energies (do magic) but the fairies have been working with it for eons and are quite adept.

Because humans in general are not kind to things they do not understand, most fairies have chosen to remain invisible to humans. And because people in general do not believe in things they cannot see, most people do not believe that fairies are real.

However, there are many forces in nature that we do not need to see to believe. Wind is a prime example: how do you know there is a breeze before seeing it ruffle the trees or brush across your face?

Of course anyone over the age of seven or eight is ridiculed for believing in things unseen. Tales of fairies – or Fairy Tales - were relegated to lighthearted bedtime stories, nothing more, and through the ages people stopped believing.

If you are reading this book, we assume that you *do* believe - and the fairies are ever so grateful for that!

Even if you have never seen a fairy and are not even sure if they exist, surely you are aware of the natural elements. Rest assured that if you are respectful of mother earth, you are honoring the fairy folk.

Keep in mind that the more time you spend in nature, the better your chances for understanding fairies and their magic.

Look deep into nature, and then you will understand everything better. - Albert Einstein

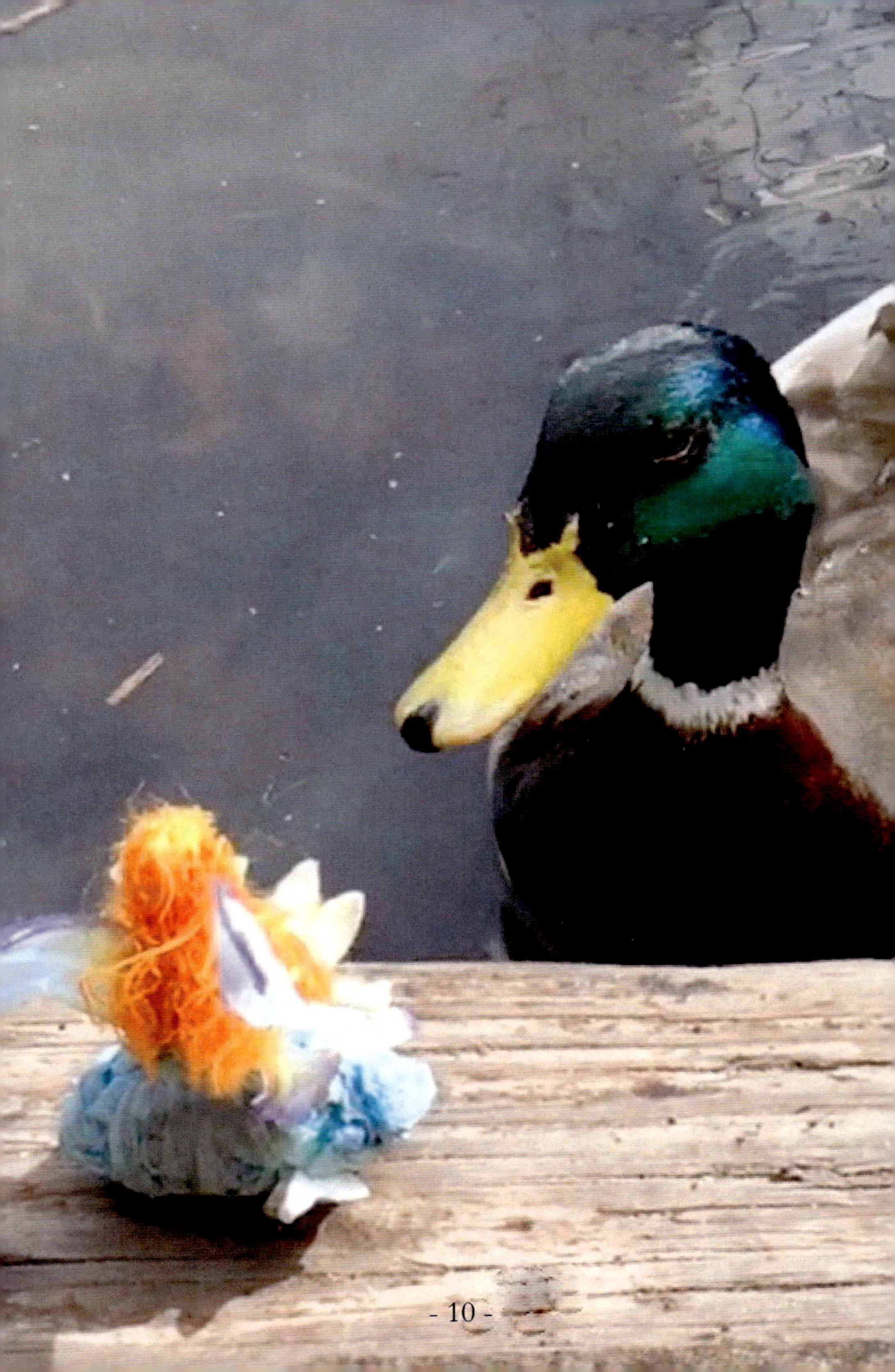

… **Do Fairies Make Good Companions?**

They had to say goodbye to their fairy because
They found it had become much too mischievous.

Just like people, fairies can be naughty or helpful, timid or bold, pleasant or unpleasant. The goal of this book is to help you keep your fairy happy and comfortable so it will be a pleasant fairy.

The remaining chapters will help you to become a great fairy keeper, but before you get to that point there are several things to understand about fairies before inviting one or more into your home.

Keep the following facts in mind before you decide if you are ready to keep a fairy:

Fairies are most definitely *not* pets. They will not be summoned like cats or dogs, and they will not perform tricks for human enjoyment. They do not like to be petted or handled. If you do get lucky enough to touch a fairy, use a very light touch, and never *ever* try to trap or contain it. And for goodness sakes, never tug at their wings!

Fairies are multi-dimensional and can appear as a dragonfly or hummingbird or even just as an invisible movement of air. Many people may never be sure if one is near.

Fairies are masters of disguise and can blend into their surroundings like chameleons. Just because they don't want to be seen doesn't mean they don't want to be near you, so never take offense.

Fairies can be very mischievous. They have been known to hide coins, keys, and lip-sticks among other things.

If a fairy is being too naughty, it is a sign they are not happy with their environment.

Fairies can turn invisible at any time. Even when they are visible they can be quiet and sneaky and hard to spot or keep track of.

Fairies tend to prefer to live in a group (also known as a flutter). They can be quite demanding when not in the presence of their own kind.

Fairies value their independence, and sometimes may come off as very aloof. But they can make excellent companions if they feel welcomed and valued in your presence.

If, after learning all these things about fairies, you feel you will make a good companion for a fairy, then a fairy will be a good companion for you.

Just remember that humans can never own fairies. If a fairy comes into your life, it is by their choice and they are free to leave at any time.

Most fairies instinctively know just when to be a part of your life and when it is time to move on.

Preparing a Place for Your Fairy

Moss and feathers, or velvets and chrome,
Many a place will a fairy call home.

Where will your fairy live?

Ideally, you should prepare a special place for your fairy well before you start looking for one to keep. This will show them that you are interested in their welfare and contentment.

A fairy place can be as simple as a shoebox filled with fairy trinkets and playthings, or as elaborate as a whole garden devoted to their pleasures.

It's best to start with a fairy door, and don't worry too much about the size. Fairies are very adept at using magic. They can change their size to enter any sized fairy door, and can make any door into a portal to a cozy home.

Although some fairies are reluctant to use their magic, so the more you can do for them the better. A door that opens is preferable to one that needs magic to open. A tree hollow that is furnished with a place to sit is preferable to an empty space needing their magic to fill.

If you are lucky enough to have a tree like this in your backyard, then you already have a fairy place! Perhaps you could add a door for their privacy, or a chair for their comfort.

Providing your fairy with their own door is good, but making them a whole fairy house will make them even happier.

There are many ways to construct fairy houses depending on your budget and skill level. You can make one from scratch using materials such as:

* Paper Mache or cardboard
* Mud or clay
* A tree log or stump
* Twigs or stones

Or you can make it easier by embellishing a ready made container such as

* An inverted plant pot
* An empty milk carton
* Glass jar or plastic bottle
* A bird cage – but only if the door is always left open.

All of these can be decorated and adorned with a fairy in mind.

This stone beach cottage was made by gluing natural found materials onto a milk carton.

For this sand covered cottage, a paper coffee cup was used and the door was folded back so it could be opened and shut.

Here are those houses placed in their natural settings using materials gathered nearby for embellishments.

This castle on the sand was created using only shells collected from the shoreline. (Held together with a little hot glue.)

After the mermaid fairies were finished exploring, it was left on the beach for the enjoyment of passing beachcombers.

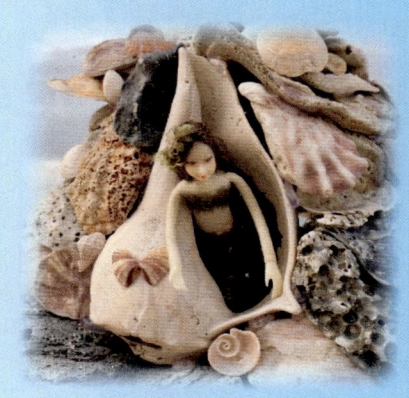

Remember that fairies are most comfortable in nature, so try to include things from all four of the earth elements like rocks (earth) and wood (fire) and seashells (water) and feathers (air).

Fairies love to be surrounded by items from their natural habitats: Forest fairies like to have moss or pinecones nearby, Garden fairies like plants and flowers, Woodland fairies love stones, etc.

Of course *all* fairies are attracted to all things that sparkle, so add some crystals or sequins, or finish off your creation with a dusting of glitter.

Someone cleverly turned a bare tree stump into a charming fairy abode.

Providing your fairy with their own house is great, but making them a whole fairy garden will make them even happier.

This is a portion of a large outdoor garden with all manner of fairy houses and fun items.

can be as small as an indoor container as a bit of your backyard.

 nts to add to the garden to keep your fairy y would be:

* A p   walkway to the door.
* A swing. Tables and benches.
* Stepping stones and patios.
* A water element, such as a pond.
* Bird baths. Potted plants.

These live-plant container gardens contain some of these elements.

The fairy houses were made from recycled plastic bottles and pieces of firewood, with doors made from polymer clay in a fairy garden class.

Here are some more gardens created by students of the class, showing just how creative you can be:

A container garden does not always have to contain live plants. Here is a tiny fairy house that is in a dry garden - decorated either with sand and succulents or dried moss.

Here is a tiny mushroom fairy house that can make a fine home for a fairy - outdoors in a natural environment or in a container garden. Succulent gardens are fine places for fairy homes.

Polymer clay is a great medium for creating fairy houses. These red door houses were all made using small plant pots as molds.

Polymer clay is also a great medium for
because it can be made into doors that open. Th
to the variety of fairy door styles. They beco
will turn any tree, block wall, or space into a f

- 25 -

Fae, the Fae Folk® fairy ambassador, travels all over the US looking for the perfect spot in which to settle down.

She narrowed the field down and picked this mossy tree for a vacation home.

Now she is going fairy chair shopping for the new place.

Here is an example of a full blown fairy forest created in the corner of a room, showing you can go as small or as big as your imagination allows.

Photo submitted through Facebook by Linda Saenz.

If your fairy garden is outdoors, don't be surprised if it attracts lots of garden creatures. Fairies don't mind sharing their spaces, because only fairies can enter a fairy door.

Once your fairy place is created, you may have fairies arriving before you know it!

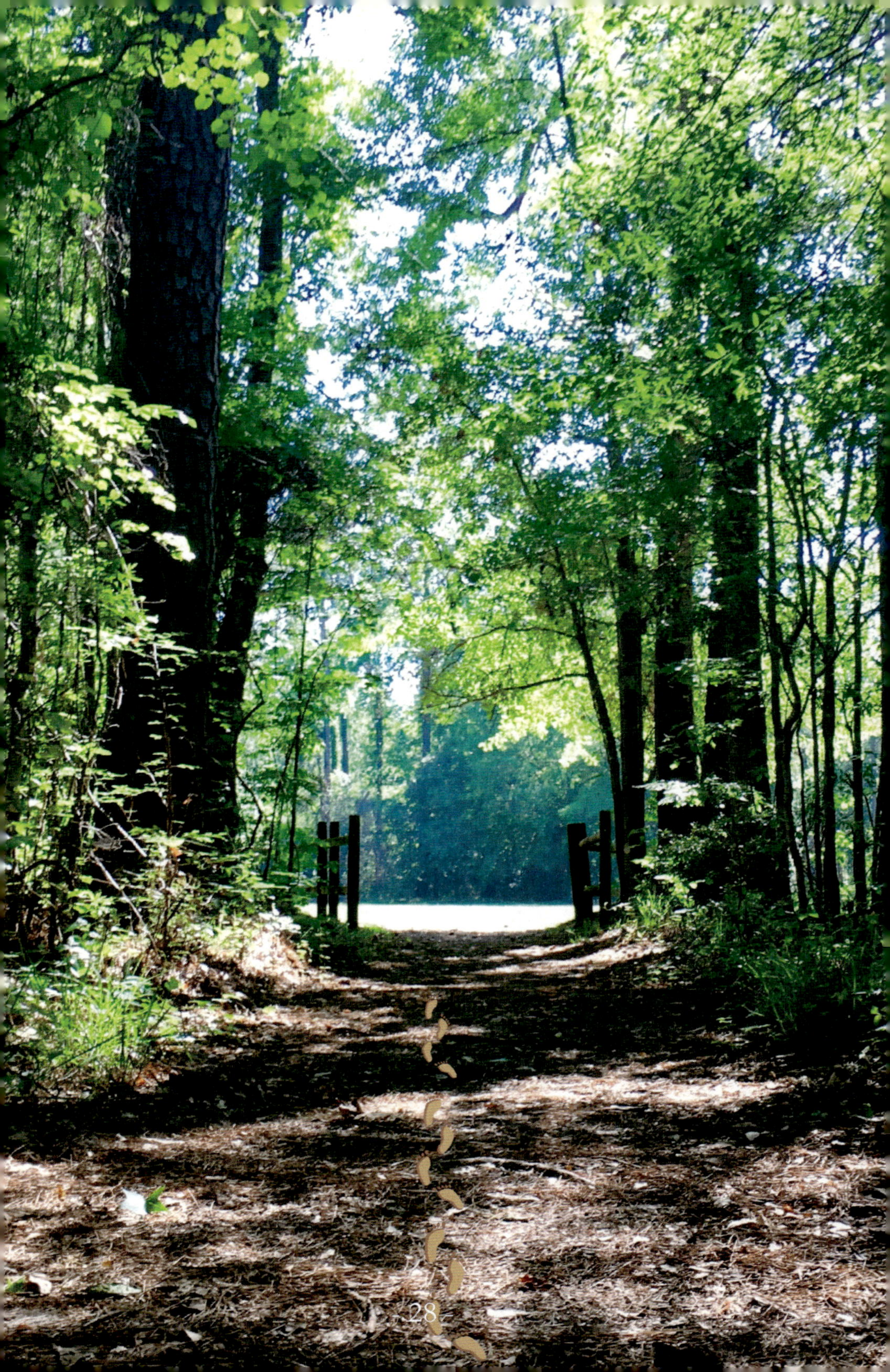

Keeping a Fairy Happy and Healthy

Music and laughter and dancing galore,
These are the standards of fairy folk lore.

Now that you've gotten a space ready for your fairy, it's time to think about what keeps a fairy happy and healthy. Remember, if they are not content in their surroundings they may get into too much mischief, or even pack up and leave.

Fairies thrive on fresh air and sunshine, so if your fairy is living indoors it's important to let them get outside every day. Going on nature walks with your fairy would please them tremendously.

Exposure to televisions, computers, cigarette smoke and cell phones will quickly make fairies sick, so limit their exposure. Again, fresh air and sunshine (or moonlight) is the best remedy if they are feeling ill.

Fairies prefer to gather their own foods from nature, like honey and nectar, but would be most appreciative if you made them tiny dishes, such as from acorns or leaves. Be wary of leaving cake crumbs or other deserts out for your fairies because processed sugar will decrease their vibrational field.

All fairies love music and dancing. They prefer harmonious tunes and love melodies; from the delicate pitter pat of rain falling, to a lively tune played on a fiddle. Fairies love to have music played for them and are especially fond of flute music.

It is not a myth that fairies can ruin their shoes from so much dancing, so if you were to make them extra shoes it would make them extremely happy.

While they love music, fairies don't however enjoy loud or sharp noises (although some fairies don't mind an occasional barking dog).

Fairy wings can be quite delicate and sensitive. They hate the age-old rumor that if you can touch a fairy's wing your wish will come true. Fairies prefer to grant wishes only to those that they feel deserve it.

Fairies love to leave gifts to show their appreciation. If you find an out-of-place feather, acorn, or a special rock, chances are it was left for you by a fairy.

Fairies also appreciate gifts from their human friends. If you leave out a shiny bead and it disappears, most likely a fairy took it home.

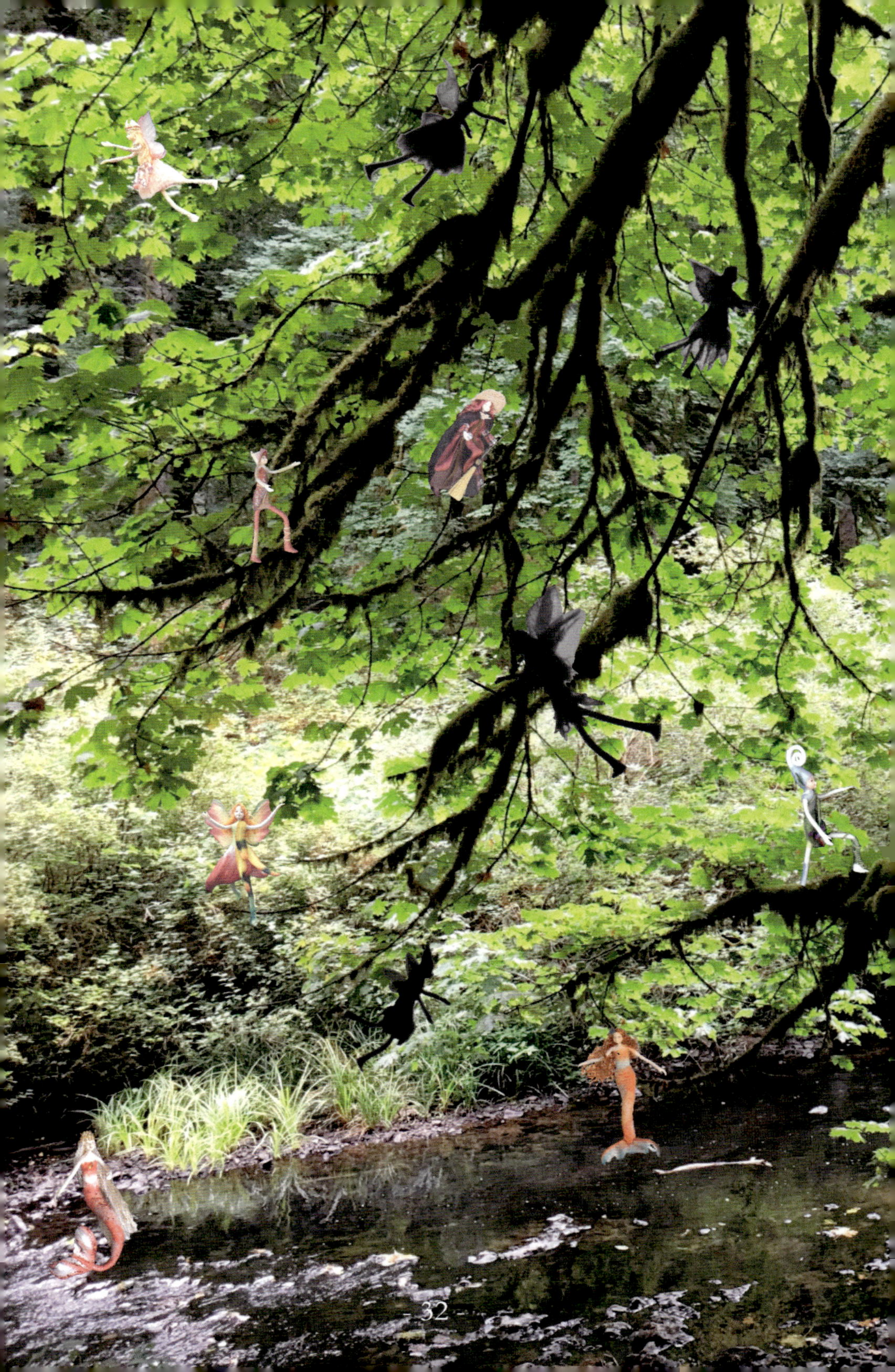

-33-

Did you find all 24 fairies hiding on the preceding pages?

Finding & Attracting Your Fairy

To discover a fairy, everyone knows:
Look where the green moss grows and the water flows.

Now that you are prepared to be a fairy keeper, have created a special place for them, and know how to keep them happy and healthy, how will you find your fairy?

That depends on the type of fairy you're looking for. There are woodland fairies, forest fairies, garden fairies, water fairies, flower fairies, etc.

Follow a trail of fireflies down a country road to look for a stardust fairy.

Look to spot a ring of mushrooms if you're looking for a woodland fairy.

Look among the flowers for a trail of ladybugs if a garden fairy is what you're looking for.

If you're looking for a water fairy or mermaid, then watch for the glittering dewdrops on a pond or lake.

Always look for signs of fairies like a string of gleaming stones or objects that mark their paths, or a circle of crushed grass where they have danced or rested.

When you find fairies (or evidence of them) in nature, you may invite them to follow you home. Some people feel a need to trap or capture fairies in cages, but that does not lead to a good relationship, so it's highly discouraged. The best way to gather a fairy friend is to let them come to you.

You have already started the process by creating a special place for the fairy.

Now you need to add some things that will attract the

type of fairy you want. Remember the four elements of nature? Each element is associated with a character trait and they are important to keep in mind if you want to attract a particular type of fairy.

Air

If you want a cerebral fairy, one who puts a lot of thought into things and can converse on many varied subjects, you will want to attract an air fairy. In addition to feathers, you can put out bells or burn incense. Light blue, white, and yellow are colors that will please them.

Water

If you're looking for an emotional bond, you'll want to make an inviting place for a water fairy. Water fairies are compassionate and intuitive. To attract them, use vessels that could contain water, such as a tiny cup from a thimble. Also put out plenty of items from water such as driftwood or polished river stones. Think of water colors such as deep blue, green and aqua to use in their environment.

Fire

If you want a high energy fairy with a lot of creative energy, then use a lot of wood (symbolizing fire) in your fairy environment. It is suggested that you do not use the obvious fire element, such as a burning candle, for it could easily singe a fairy's wing. Keep in mind that fire fairies can be the most temperamental. Red and orange are the favorite colors of fire fairies.

Earth

Earth fairies are quite practical, loyal and very nurturing. They are easily attracted with crystals or stones. Remember that salt is a natural crystal, and some earth fairies flip for a bit of pink rock salt. Colors to use to invite earth fairies would be greens and browns.

Of course, because fairies are attracted to all things shiny and sparkly, putting out glitter (also known as pixie dust) will get their attention.

Because fairies are multi-dimensional creatures and masters of disguise, how will you know when one appears?

They may show up as dragonflies, or birds, or butterflies.

Welcome them all!

Some signs you have become a fairy keeper:

* You will see tiny footprints in places.
* There will be tiny nature gifts left for you.
* You will feel a soft breeze on your cheek.
* Things in your fairy garden will be re-arranged.
* Mushrooms will pop up in your yard.
* You will hear a faint humming in your ear.
* You will find a trail of glitter or rhinestones or other sparkly items they left behind to mark their trails.

If you've followed the suggestions given here, it's only a matter of time until the right fairy shows up in your special fairy place and lets you become a fairy keeper.

You may even attract more than one!

How Do You Communicate With a Fairy?

Small tinkling bells? Is that what you hear?
It probably means a fairy is near.

Now that you've become a fairy keeper and attracted the fairy or fairies that you've wished for, it's important to know how to communicate with them.

Fairies don't like loud or sudden noises, so you should only speak to them in hushed voices. Always, *always* speak softly and kindly to them. They are very sensitive creatures and they have exceptionally good hearing - especially the varieties with the large pointed ears.

To have a fairy talk back to you, you have to be a very careful listener. To hear them or get messages from them, you may have to sit quietly for a long time. Fairies generally only speak telepathically to humans, so when they speak to you, you hear it only as thoughts or feelings. Some may never hear a fairy speak, but that's okay. Keep talking softly to them and tell them of your hopes and dreams, and they will always listen and understand.

When fairies speak among themselves, it can sound like a faint and melodious buzzing.

Never let language become a barrier in getting to know your fairy. They are lovers of play and games and are willing to interact with you if given the chance.

Try playing hide and seek games with them – for that is their favorite and they are quite good at it. Of course they have the upper hand with their ability to vanish from our sight! So try playing with objects such as hiding a button to see if it will end up in their fairy home.

Music is also a way to intuitively interact with your fairy. If you are a musician, so much the better, for your fairy will love to listen to you play. If not, try playing different types of songs or sounds (like wind chimes or water sounds) and see if you notice a positive change in your environment. This may be your fairy communicating its pleasure to you.

14

What to Expect After Your Fairy Arrives

It can be such a magical thing,
To stumble upon a fairy ring.

Once you have invited a fairy into your home, you will begin to notice subtle differences.

You may begin to hear more birds singing. This might be because you're noticing them more or it may be because more of them have moved into your neighborhood along with the fairy.

You may find that you start whistling or humming to yourself more often. Your fairy will appreciate this as they enjoy harmonies.

If it's springtime, you will probably be aware of more wild flowers blooming than normal.

If you grow flowers, prepare to be impressed with larger and more plentiful blooms. Fairies love to help your garden grow. Don't forget to leave a flower on your fairy's doorstep to thank them for their attention to your gardening efforts.

If you garden for food, you will probably notice that the produce you harvest has more flavor than ever. And if you attract a certain type of witch fairy (also know as a kitchen witch) they will inspire you to create the most delectable recipes.

Fairies and other Creatures

You may observe more insects or critters in your area. Dragonflies, caterpillars, butterflies, toads, ladybugs, grasshoppers, hummingbirds, and even snails are all attracted to your fairy's energy. If you're finding creatures you're not fond of – spiders for instance – then just politely ask your fairy to tell them to stay away.

> *Note: Remember bugs are creatures too and your fairy would be appalled if it ever saw you smash one.*

. If you have horses or other large animals, you might notice them being distracted by something you can't see. It is probably the fairy playing with them.

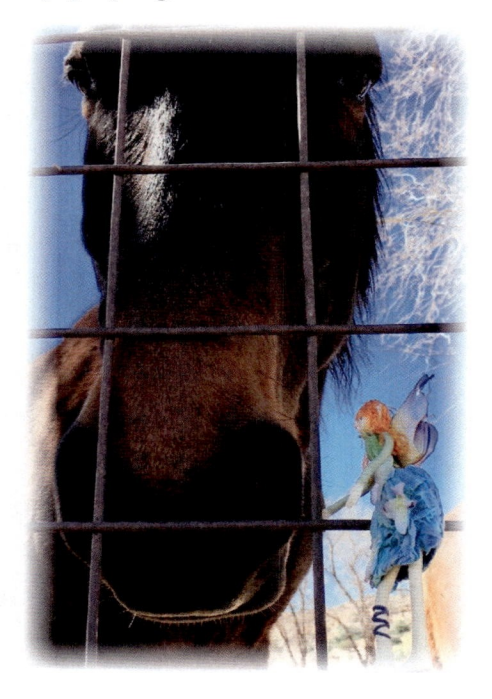

Cats usually don't care about fairies living in your home, but some fairies adore kittens, so if your cat has a litter, don't be surprised to see a fairy nearby.

Dogs are especially attuned to fairies because of their excellent hearing. (Their hearing frequency is twice as high as humans.) There are a only few fairies that are frightened of dogs, so if you feel like your fairy doesn't like your dog, make sure you keep the fairy protected so it doesn't feel threatened. Otherwise, don't be surprised if your dog seems more playful, for most fairies love to interact with them.

Naming Your Fairy

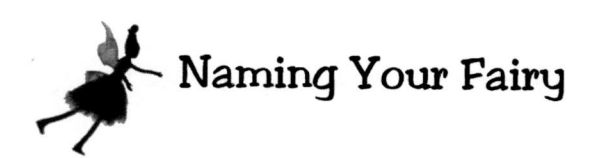

Is your name Polly? Fido? Missy? I asked.
"It is Rumplestiltskin," he shouted, aghast.

All fairies have their own names. But their human friends may not always know what it is — or be able to speak it.

If you don't intuitively know what the name of your fairy is, they will not mind if you come up with a name to call them. If they don't respond to the name you've given them, it doesn't mean they don't like it - fairies just don't like to be summoned on command.

When looking for a proper fairy name you might want to use an adjective like Affable or Joyful. Perhaps you can look up Celtic or Latin versions of common words. For instance, if you think your fairy would like the name Happy, you might also want to consider Sona (Celtic) or Felix (Latin).

You should always look to nature for inspiration. Keep in mind your fairy's favorite element or habitat when deciding on a name.

Water fairies like names associated with oceans, fish, lakes or rivers. Brook is a good example of a body of water and a great fairy name. You might want to add letters to make it Brookie or Brooks.

Other possibilities are Dolphina (an A added to dolphin), Coral, or Rivers (an S added to river).

Air fairies like names associated with weather and movement in the skies, such as Stormy, Sunny, Windy, or Cloudy. Don't be afraid to change letters making Cloudy – Cloudie.

Stardust fairies love names taken from the heavens such as Star or Venus.

Tree names are popular fairy names for earth fairies (Willow), highland fairies (Aspen) and forest fairies (Piney).

Think of campfire terms for fire fairies: Marshmallow, Ashes (or Ashley), Flicker, or Ember.

Jewel fairies, a subgroup of earth fairies, like to be named after precious stones like Ruby(ie) or Emerald(a).

The names are endless for flower fairies: Daisy, Rose, Violet, Periwinkle.

Fairy names can also be inspired by their colors. If you see that your fairy has warm colors like reds, oranges, and yellows, then perhaps Sunset is a fitting name. Maybe the name of an interesting color is appropriate like Crimson or Indigo.

You can always look to history or literature for famous fairy names. Oberon and Titania were the king and queen of the fairies in Shakespeare's "Midsummer Night's Dream" and other fairy names from that play were Mustardseed, Puck, and Cobweb.

And of course there is always Tinker or Bell!

Fairies are androgynous for the most part, but you might feel that your fairy has a female (yin) energy, or a masculine (yang) energy and you can name them accordingly.

Naming a fairy should come from a gut feeling. Just like in all aspects of life, you should always trust your intuition.

Rules of Fairy Keeping

Always be as nice as nice can be
And you'll stay a pal to your fairy

Do not expect your fairy to use its magic to fix your life. Remember they are beings of nature.

Do not expect your fairy to show itself 24/7. Respect their privacy as they will respect yours.

Do not feel the need to explain your fairy friend to those you feel just don't understand. Your fairy will never make itself visible to those people anyway.

Just remember the main rule of fairies:

You must *Believe!*

*Believe in Fairies
They hope you do
make a wish
it might come true!*

Dearest Reader,

Thank you for joining along in the adventure of this book. We hope you enjoyed it.

We would be ever so grateful if you would leave an honest review on Amazon.com. We'd love to know your thoughts on the existence of fairies and their magic.

We'd also love for you to post pictures of your fairies or fairy places using the tag #faefolkworld.

Feel free to contact us at 559-972-7780 or by email at joysfate@sbcglobal.net.

Peace & Love, Joy & Tom

The power of imagination makes us infinite.

- John Muir

About the Authors

Tom and Joy McGuire collaborated on this book about fairies in the hopes that it will move more people to be aware of their natural surroundings and to have an appreciation for Mother Earth by getting outside to commune with nature.

It is also their hope that it will ignite the imagination of the readers and remind them to always keep a childlike wonder.

Currently, they have embarked on a permanent vacation, touring the USA while living full time in an RV. Joy is an award winning novelist and is currently blogging about their adventures at **www.rightlaners.com.**

This book was brought to you by:

Fae Folk® World

You can also find us on:

Thank You!

Made in the USA
Middletown, DE
21 August 2023